P9-CRZ-857

WORD BIRD'S
FALL WORDS

by Jane Belk Moncure
illustrated by Linda Hohag

THE
CHILD'S
WORLD

ELGIN, ILLINOIS 60120

Distributed by Childrens Press, 1224 West Van Buren Street,
Chicago, Illinois 60607.

Library of Congress Cataloging in Publication Data

Moncure, Jane Belk.
    Word Bird's fall words.

    (Word house words for early birds)
    Summary: Word Bird puts words about fall in his word
house—leaves, playground, football, Pilgrims, monsters,
and others.
    1. Vocabulary—Juvenile literature.   2. Autumn—
Juvenile literature.   [1. Vocabulary.   2. Autumn]
I. Hohag, Linda, ill.   II. Title.   III. Series: Moncure,
Jane Belk.   Word house words for early birds.
PE1449.M528   1985   428.1   85-5935
ISBN 0-89565-308-7

1 2 3 4 5 6 7 8 9 10 11 12 R 91 90 89 88 87 86 85

WORD BIRD'S FALL WORDS

Word Bird made a ...

word house.

"I will put fall words
in my house," he said.

He put in these words –

school bus

lunch box

red

yellow

orange

brown

leaves

9

football

acorns

squirrels

caterpillar

cocoon

Columbus finds a new land.

Niña
Pinta
Santa Maria

Columbus Day

17

wild geese

pumpkins

Halloween

jack-o'-lantern

monsters

trick or treat

Thanksgiving pies

Thanksgiving turkey

Mayflower

Pilgrims

Indians

tepee

school bus

caterpillar

lunch box

cocoon

leaves

Columbus Day

OCTOBER 12

football

wild geese

acorns

squirrels

pumpkins

hese fall words with WORD BIRD ?

Halloween

Thanksgiving turkey

ack-o'-lantern

Mayflower

monsters

Pilgrims

trick or treat

Indians

hanksgiving pies

tepee

You can make a fall word house. You can put Word Bird's words in your house and read them too.

32